The Little Kitten

A Random House PICTUREBACK®

The Little Kitten

Story by **Judy Dunn**

Photographs by **Phoebe Dunn**

Random House 🏠 New York

Text Copyright © 1983 by Judy Dunn Spangenberg. Photographs Copyright © 1983 by Phoebe Dunn. All rights reserved under International and Pan-American Copyright Conventions. Published in the United States by Random House, Inc., New York, and simultaneously in Canada by Random House of Canada Limited, Toronto.

Library of Congress Cataloging in Publication Data: Dunn, Judy. The little kitten. SUMMARY: Jenny's new kitten is always wandering off and getting into mischief until she thinks of a unique solution for keeping an eye on him. [1. Cats—Fiction] I. Dunn, Phoebe, ill. II. Title. PZ7.D92158Lg 1982 [E] 82-16711 ISBN: 0-394-85818-2 (pbk.); 0-394-95818-7 (lib. bdg.) Manufactured in the United States of America

Jenny's cat was restless. It was time for her kittens to be born.

She looked in the barn for a comfortable spot to have her kittens, but the straw was much too scratchy. She prowled all over the house and yard. But nothing seemed to suit her.

So Jenny made a soft bed for her cat in the bottom drawer of her bureau. That night six fluffy kittens were born there.

Jenny's cat was a good mother. She nursed her kittens when they were hungry and washed them with her rough, pink tongue.

At first the kittens seemed to sleep all day. But in a few weeks they were tumbling all over one another. When the mother cat wanted a little peace, she crouched under the drawer.

One little kitten was more curious than the others. He was the first to try his wobbly legs.

He was the first to peek over the edge of the drawer.

And he was the first to climb out of the bureau. PLOP! He fell to the floor. But Jenny found him and scooped him up before he had a chance to get into trouble.

Jenny's mother promised that she could keep one of the kittens. They would find new homes for the others.

Jenny loved every one of the kittens, but she loved the curious kitten most of all.

"You're my favorite!" she said to the kitten.

"Meow," the kitten answered softly.

Jenny made a bed for her kitten in a special basket. The kitten tried it out right away. He was still little and needed lots of naps. When he woke up, he was ready to go exploring.

The curious kitten scampered through the house. He found Father's sneakers and tried to squeeze inside. But already he was too big to fit. The kitten was growing very fast.

Soon the kitten was old enough to drink milk from a dish. At first he didn't know what to do. He stepped right into it! Milk stuck to his paws and dripped from his chin.

"Oh, what a pickle you're in!" said Jenny when she saw the milky kitten.

Saying that gave her an idea. "I'm going to call you Pickle," she told her kitten. It turned out to be a very good name for him.

The curious kitten got into one pickle after another. One day he wanted to see what was inside a can of flour.

What a mess that made! Pickle looked so funny that Jenny didn't even mind cleaning up after him.

Jenny played with her kitten every day. One night she gave him a catnip mouse. It made the kitten do silly things.

First he sniffed the mouse. . . .

Then he batted it . . .
and clawed it . . . and licked
it . . . and chewed it and
rolled it around on the floor!

Soon the mouse was in
shreds and the kitten was all
tired out.

Jenny let Pickle sleep on
her bed just this once. The
little kitten curled up beside
her and purred. He was
happy to be with Jenny.

One sunny day Jenny took her kitten outdoors. She
wanted him to keep her company while she planted some
flowers. Pickle tried to see everything she was doing. He
kept getting in the way.

Finally Jenny picked
up the kitten and put
him in a flowerpot.
"Now stay there,"
she scolded.

But Pickle was too curious
to stay anywhere for long.
He jumped out of the
flowerpot and set off on an
adventure.

Pickle wandered into the meadow, where he felt safe
in the tall grass. He hardly knew where to look first.
There were so many sights and sounds and smells that
were new to him.

He discovered a turtle
sunning itself on a rock . . .
a praying mantis waiting to
catch an insect for lunch . . .
and two baby squirrels
climbing a tree and
chattering to each other.

A baby rabbit was hiding under a mushroom. The rabbit sat very still and hoped the kitten wouldn't notice him.

Wild strawberries grew in the meadow. So did lots of flowers. The kitten watched a caterpillar inch up the stem of a Queen Anne's lace.

Beyond the meadow Pickle climbed onto a woodpile. He found lots of hiding places in it.

Then he tried to squeeze into an empty woodchuck hole but got stuck halfway!

"Meow, meow!" he cried.

Jenny finally heard him and came to his rescue.

"Please don't get into any more trouble," she begged.

After that she held her kitten very close whenever she took him outdoors.

Pickle liked Jenny's attention. But he liked to explore
even better. It wasn't long before he slipped away again.
This time he practiced walking on the orchard fence.
He had a good sense of balance, so he didn't fall once.

Then Pickle scrambled up
an apple tree. Climbing up
was easy, but he was too
frightened to climb back
down.

"Meow," he called.
"Mee-ow-w-w."

"Oh, Pickle, you're in a pickle again!" said Jenny when she found him.

She dragged a box out to the tree and gently helped the little kitten down.

"Now don't go off again!" said Jenny.

Pickle snuggled up to her and purred. He seemed to be saying that he'd had enough exploring.

But the very next day he was off again! Jenny took him to a birthday party, and when the children weren't watching, Pickle wandered away. They finally found him snoozing in the doghouse.

"What *am* I going to do with you?" Jenny asked her kitten. Suddenly she had an idea. . . .

"Now you can't hide from me, Pickle!"